Cats on the Prowl

A Cat Detective Cozy Mystery Series

BOOK ONE

Nancy C. Davis

Copyright 2015 Collins Collective

All rights reserved.

No part of this book may be reproduced in any form or by any electronic or mechanical means including information storage and retrieval systems, without permission in writing from the author.

This book is a work of fiction. Names, characters, places, and incidents either are products of the author's imagination or are used fictitiously. Any resemblance to actual persons, living or dead, events, or locales is entirely coincidental.

CONTENTS

CHAPTER 1 1

CHAPTER 2 17

CHAPTER 3 31

CHAPTER 4 47

CHAPTER 5 63

CHAPTER 6 83

CHAPTER 7 101

CHAPTER 8 117

CHAPTER 9 129

CHAPTER 10 147

CHAPTER 11 163

CHAPTER 1

Willow, a fluffy white Persian, jumped up onto Sergeant Carl Ridout's desk and pushed the papers out of the way with her paw. "I've never seen such an untidy man. I don't know how he keeps track of anything in this mess."

Nat, the big tabby tom, lifted his head from Detective Naya Wesley's chair and chuckled. The sound rumbled out of his chest in a deep purr. "He doesn't keep track of anything. That's exactly why he does it."

"Then how does he solve his cases?" Willow asked. "He's a police sergeant. He's supposed to be catching criminals."

"He doesn't catch any criminals," Nat told her. "Haven't you figured that out yet? It's Naya who solves the cases. I don't think Sergeant Ridout has solved a case in the seven years I've been living here at the Nelson Police Station. I've followed the details of every case, and I've found it very clear who actually solves them."

"How can he be a police sergeant, then?" Willow asked. "Hasn't anyone noticed he doesn't do any work?"

"I didn't say he doesn't do any work," Nat explained. "He does a lot of work. Oh, my, does he ever do a lot of work! It's just not the kind of work that would solve cases."

"What does he do?" Willow asked.

"You've seen him," Nat shot back. "You've been here almost a year now, ever since Naya found you in the drain behind the station. What a sight you were that day. I can still remember it. You looked like a half-drowned rat, with your hair all stuck to your head. We didn't know if you would survive. You looked like something the cat dragged in."

Willow sniffed. "You don't have to rub it in. I remember it as well as you do. I didn't think I was coming to live at the police station to poke my nose into the confidential case files of the Homicide Department."

Nat licked his paw and cleaned the side of his face. "I didn't think I was coming to poke my nose into confidential files, either. But when you've been here as long as I have, you can't help but notice who does what. Carl sits at his desk and pushes paper from one side to the other until sweat pours off his forehead. He curses under his breath and mutters about how he doesn't know what the world is coming to."

"I've seen that," Willow replied. "That's why I assumed he got a lot done."

"He gets a lot of filing done," Nat told her. "Then you look at Naya. She sits at her desk, but she doesn't make a sound. She doesn't pick up one piece of paper and put it in a pile with a dozen other papers. She sits there for an hour or more, going over every detail until she finds out what she wants to know. Then she moves on to the next one and does the same thing. That's how she finds the clues to solve cases."

"If you're right," Willow remarked, "it's a good thing Sergeant Ridout has Naya for a partner. He could take the credit for her solving the cases."

"Naya wouldn't have lasted ten seconds on the police force if she hadn't had Carl for a partner," Nat told her. "Naya was a raw recruit from the Academy when they started working together. Carl listened to her and believed in her when she solved her first case. She would have lost heart and quit the force without his support."

"Were you here back then?" Willow asked.

"I was here," he rumbled. "I've seen dozens of recruits come and go in my seven years. Naya has only been here three years, and Carl has been here five years. You watch them together. Naya comes up with the clues, but it's Carl who pushes the case to its conclusion. She's the brains and he's the brawn. They're a perfect team."

Willow glanced down at the papers around her feet. "I guess I have a lot to learn about police work. I don't know what half these papers say."

"That's because you can't read," Nat pointed out. "If you want to find out what's going on with human beings, that's the first thing you have to learn."

"How am I going to do that?" she asked.

"I'll teach you," he replied. "It's not complicated when you get the hang of it."

"How did you learn?" she asked. "Did someone teach you?"

"No one taught me," he replied. "I figured it out for myself. I wanted to understand why people thought these papers were so important. It took me a lot longer to learn by myself than it'll take me to teach you, but never mind. You'll get the hang of it, and then you can help me solve cases, too."

Willow's head shot up. "You solve cases, too?"

"Of course," he exclaimed. "I wouldn't be much of a police cat if I didn't. I've been living at the police station for seven years. I've got to earn my keep somehow."

"I would love to solve criminal cases," Willow cried. "How do you do it?"

Nat sat up on the chair and faced her. "The first thing you've got to do—which you don't do now—is to start paying attention around here. You can't just lie around and purr and expect to become a real police cat. You can't just curl up on Naya's lap and go to sleep. You have to listen to what she says."

Willow pretended to sneeze. "I don't just curl up on Naya's lap and go to sleep. I'm not lazy. People keep cats for comfort. That's the service I provide in exchange for my keep."

"Now, just listen to what I have to say," Nat returned. "I'm not saying curling up on Naya's lap and closing your eyes isn't a good thing to do. I know giving people comfort is a big part of being a cat, although I don't really do that sort of thing myself. I'm a tom. My job is singing on fences and spraying in their gardens. I'm just saying that, when you curl up on Naya's lap and close your eyes, you only pretend to sleep. In reality, you keep awake and listen."

"But they don't talk about much of anything," Willow replied. "They mostly complain about the Captain and the Union and a bunch of other things

I don't understand."

"Those things you don't understand are the details of their cases," Nat told her. "That's why you have to listen. While you're learning to read the reports and letters and documents, you can pick up all kinds of information from listening to their conversations. That's how I solve my cases."

"Can you really solve cases by listening to their conversations and reading all these papers?" Willow waved her paw at the clutter on Carl's desk. "Wow, Nat, I'm sorry I didn't realize you were so smart."

"Don't judge a book by it's cover," he replied. "But I don't solve cases by reading papers and listening to their conversations. That's just the beginning. Once you've gleaned all the information you can from the papers and listening to them talk, you have to go out into the field."

"You mean like going out catching mice and crickets and that sort of thing?" Willow asked. "I was never very good at that. I get foxtails in my fur and grass in my ears. The last time I went, I had to spend six hours at the vet getting a foxtail taken out of my ear. It cost my owner seven hundred dollars, and she never let me outside again."

"I don't mean that," Nat explained. "When I say the field, I don't mean grass and mice. I'm talking about hitting the bricks and hunting down your clues. You have to track down your suspects and find more clues and information. You won't solve a case sitting behind a desk."

Willow put her head to one side. "Is that what Naya and Carl do all day? I thought they just went out together for a ride in the car."

"They go their own way," Nat replied, "and I go mine. I have my own way of getting information. The good thing is, a cat can go places and listen to things a person can't. Two crooks will tell each other their life stories with a cat sitting right in front of them. They'll reveal information to a cat they wouldn't reveal to their own mothers. That's how you catch them."

"But how can finding out what they did help you catch them?" Willow asked. "They might talk in front of a cat, but you can't jump up and arrest them. You can't handcuff them and throw them in the county lock-up."

Nat strutted along the edge of Naya's desk. "That's where human beings come in very handy. You can't arrest them, but Carl and Naya can. You give them your information, and they arrest the criminals for you."

"How do you give them your information?" Willow asked. "Do you write them a note?"

"Write them a note!" Nat snorted. "I should think not. I am a cat. I do not write. Reading is one thing, but I wouldn't stoop so low as to write. Write! Ha!"

"How do you do it, then?" Willow asked. "How can you give them information?"

Nat stood up tall and straight. The moonlight streaming through the police station window stretched his shadow across the carpet. "That, my dear, is the great secret of the cat race. We find a way to draw Naya's attention to the evidence, but we must be discreet. We can't let her know we found out the crucial piece of the puzzle to solve the case. We must do it in a way that preserves the illusion that Naya solved the case herself."

"Why do we have to do that?" Willow shot back. "If we solved the case, we should take the credit."

"And how, exactly, would we do that?" Nat demanded. "How do you think it would work if the world found out cats could read and solve criminal cases? How do you think humans would react if they finally got it through their heads that we could understand their conversations? The world would be in turmoil within hours. It would never work."

"I don't know," Willow argued. "My owner used to watch a show on TV about a boy who had a dog who helped him catch criminals. The dog was called Lassie. No one gave that dog a second thought."

"That's a TV show," Nat replied. "And it's about a dog, not a cat. Dogs are different. People can believe all kinds of things about a dog, or even a fictional cat. But real cats? I don't think so. It works just fine for them to think of us as harmless pets. They wouldn't be very happy if they knew the truth about us."

Willow gazed out the window at the moon. "I know what you mean, although I don't agree. People enjoy a certain ignorance about what their cats really think and understand. They don't appreciate having those ideas contradicted. They get very snotty if anyone tells them they're wrong about anything."

"So you can understand," Nat went on, "how these people would feel if they knew their cats were solving their cases for them. These are professional police detectives. They're supposed to put the evidence together. They are not supposed to rely on cats to do it for them."

"I see." Willow jumped down and joined Nat on Naya's desk. "So when can we start?"

"Right now." Nat turned and put his paw down on the big calendar in front of him. "This is your first lesson. Do you see that pointed shape right there? That is the first thing you have to learn. That is the letter A."

CHAPTER 2

The police station door opened, and Willow sat up on the couch. She forced herself to sit still, even though every fiber of her being screamed to race across the room and jump into Naya Wesley's arms. But Nat wouldn't approve. She had to act like a regular cat. She had to keep up the pretense that she was completely oblivious to the human activity going on around her.

Willow glanced at the bundle of woolen blankets crumpled behind the water cooler. Nat never twitched a whisker. No one would guess he was awake and taking in every detail.

Naya and Carl Ridout entered the police station amid the busy hum of voices, phones ringing, and computers pinging at every desk. No one paid any attention to the cats.

Naya wore a tight-fitting brown leather jacket with a wooly collar over her tailored white button-down shirt. Her tight blue jeans ran down into knee-high brown leather boots. Carl wore a rumpled blue suit that barely fit around his massive shoulders. Scuff marks and dried mud soiled his shoes, and a rim of sweat darkened his collar and the cuffs of his sleeves.

Naya pulled out her chair, but she didn't sit down. "I'm just saying it doesn't make sense. Why would Jason Dempsey say he wasn't there when we all know he was? Why would he lie about it?"

"Why do you have to read so much into

everything?" Carl shot back. "You know how people get when they have to answer questions from the police. They'll say anything that pops into their heads. Maybe he thought he had to come up with some reason why he wasn't there. Maybe he thought we would suspect him if we thought he was there. Who knows?"

"Come on, Carl," Naya chided. "We already knew he was there. Him lying about it would make us suspect him."

"But he doesn't know that, does he?" Carl pointed out. "People don't think the same way about these things as homicide detectives. All they can think is run and hide. I've seen it a thousand times. He got scared, and he lied. No big deal."

Naya shook her head. "You can't convince me of that. He was scheduled to work this morning, and his girlfriend saw him leave the house. The clerk at the drive-through saw him park in the employee parking lot behind the Morningside Bakery, and we found the charred remains of the time clock in the fire. The imprint of his time card is the last imprint on the tape before the place went up in smoke."

"But don't you see?" Carl asked. "That just proves he didn't set that fire. He wouldn't have clocked himself in right before the place went up in flames. If he planned to tell everyone he wasn't anywhere near the bakery when it burned down, he wouldn't have clocked in at all. He would have set the fire from somewhere outside the building and beat a hasty retreat. Clocking in isn't the behavior of a would-be arsonist and murderer. He didn't have time to light the fire before the whole place went up. He was lucky to get out of the bakery with his life."

"You're not thinking clearly, Carl." Naya rummaged through the papers on her desk. "Where is it? Oh, here it is. Now, let's see. Yes. Right here. This is the insurance policy on the bakery. It clearly states the building was stucco on the outside. Jason couldn't light the fire from outside. He had to go inside to light the fire, and the best way he could do that was to wait until he was scheduled to work. He clocked in, and once inside, he set the fire and ran away."

"Then how do you explain him lying about his whereabouts?" Carl asked. "He couldn't be so stupid as to expect us to believe he really wasn't there."

Naya grinned at her big partner. "Maybe he

thought he could count on a loveable cop like you giving him a break. Maybe he had some other reason to hide his actions. Or maybe, like you say, he just got scared and said the wrong thing."

Carl sat down at his desk and picked up a stack of papers. "The good news is that we have a chance to question him more thoroughly later today. We're also questioning the bakery owner's widow. She might have a motive to kill her husband."

"Josephine Avino might have a motive to kill her husband, Roy," Naya pointed out. "But she had no opportunity. She didn't work at the bakery. There's no evidence she was there this morning."

Carl held up his index finger. "That's what she wants us to believe. Just because she wasn't clocked in doesn't mean she wasn't there. Her husband was there, and Jason was there. She could have walked through the open kitchen door anytime she wanted to."

"Don't you think Jason would have told us if there was another person in the bakery?" Naya asked. "He could have deflected the blame for the fire onto Josephine. Betrayed wife kills philandering husband. It's the perfect set-up."

Carl held up his hands. "Well, you've blown my tidy little theory to smithereens. Thank you very much. Now I don't know who to believe."

Naya sat down across from him and bent over her paperwork. "Let's not over-think things. We just started working on this case, and we've got a lot of work to do before we're done."

Willow listened to their conversation with every whisker alert. After the detectives fell silent, she sauntered across the station room as calmly as she dared. She tiptoed up to Nat's blanket bed and stepped over him. She missed her footing and accidentally stepped on his leg. Her paw rolled off and she toppled over onto him.

He growled under his breath, but he gave no indication of even noticing her. Willow curled up next to him. "Can we go out into the field now? We could go see the burned-down building and have a look around."

"Not just yet," Nat mumbled. "We don't want to miss them questioning the employee and the owner's widow. We'll stick around for that. We might pick up some details we need when we go out to view the scene of the crime."

Willow peeped with excitement. "The scene of the crime! I'm getting to be a real police cat!"

"Calm down," Nat hissed. "You don't want to blow our cover. The first job of the police cat is to keep quiet and listen. Bide your time and use your head. We don't want to run off all over the place when the case just got started. Like Naya said, we have a long way to go yet."

Three hours later, Carl wiped the sweat off his forehead and took a brown paper bag out of his desk drawer. "Lunch time. Then we'll get to questioning the suspects."

He put his meaty paw into his bag and pulled out a limp sandwich wrapped in plastic wrap. He stuffed the sandwich into his mouth and swallowed it almost in one bite. He crumpled up the bag and tossed it into his waste paper basket. Then he turned back to his work.

Naya took a stacking lunch box of shining

stainless steel from the shoulder bag under her desk and set it out in front of her. She unclipped it and set the stacking pieces in a tasteful arrangement on top of her desk calendar. She opened one section after another and took out a tiny bamboo fork.

She started eating noodles out of one section while she gazed out the window in deep thought. Carl muttered over his papers at the desk across from her. After she finished her noodles, she moved on to another section of her lunch box and started eating a salad. She took out a handful of carrot sticks.

Carl ignored the crunching as long as he could. Then he dropped his papers with an exasperated gasp. "I don't know how you can live on that rabbit food. You'll fade away to nothing eating that stuff."

Naya smiled across the desk at her partner. "We

have the same conversation every lunchtime, Carl. I'm eating a lot more over here than you are. Don't you get hungry later in the day on just a sandwich?"

Carl shrugged. "Sure, but I'm trying to lose weight. You look like you could use a few pounds."

Naya chuckled. "No one ever lost weight by cutting macronutrients. You lose weight by boosting your metabolism, and you can only do that by increasing your muscle mass. If you want to lose weight, you actually have to eat more, not less."

Carl shook his finger at her. "Don't try to confuse me with all that technical talk. I've eaten the same sandwich for twenty years, and...."

Naya put her lunchbox back together and wiped her mouth on a cotton handkerchief from her pocket. "You don't have to tell me. You've eaten the same sandwich for twenty years and you're not about to change now."

"Why should I change?" Carl shot back. "It works for me."

"It doesn't really work for you if you're trying to lose weight, does it?" Naya pointed out. "Besides, if you ate more, you wouldn't be such an intolerable ogre about three o'clock in the afternoon."

Carl stiffened. "Who said I'm an intolerable ogre at three o'clock in the afternoon?"

"I did," Naya replied. "I'm your partner, and I've seen you crash at the same time every day after eating the same sandwich for lunch. I'm here to tell you it doesn't work for you, for me or for anyone else. I don't know how your wife Sandra puts up with you."

Carl looked away. "It works fine for her because I hit the drive-through on the way home."

Naya nodded. "That explains why you're not losing weight."

Carl jerked his head toward the door. "Josephine Avino is here."

CHAPTER 3

Naya put her lunchbox away and the two detectives stood up. "I'll take her down to the interrogation room. You bring Jason when he gets here."

Willow nudged Nat with her nose. "Now what are we going to do? I thought we were going to listen in on the questioning."

"Stay calm," Nat told her, "and follow my lead."

He stood up and stretched his legs. He yawned and turned a complete circle in their nest before he stepped out into the station room. He looked around and set to work to clean his whiskers.

Willow watched with a pattering heart. Naya shook hands with a lady in a faux fur coat and a bejeweled handbag hanging from her elbow. Stiletto heels glittered on her feet, and sheer panty hose covered her legs under her crisp polyester skirt. Naya ushered her toward the stairs and disappeared.

Willow would have run after them if Nat hadn't stood up at that moment and trotted out of the room. He turned the corner after Naya and Mrs Avino. Willow waited another moment just to make sure no one was watching. Then she scampered through the door, too.

Naya opened a blank brown door in a nondescript hallway and waved Josephine Avino inside. Nat slipped into the room between her legs. Neither woman noticed him at all. Naya flipped on the light and turned to close the door. At that moment, Willow skidded to a stop and bumped her nose on the door as it closed in her face. She mewed up at Naya.

Naya yanked the door open and looked down at the fluffy Persian cat. "Do you want to come in, sweetie?" She held the door open, and Willow pranced past.

Jo Avino made a face. "What do you keep those cats around for?"

Naya sat down across from her. "They make people much more comfortable when it comes to talking to the police about a situation like this. See? She's jumping up into your lap. She understands you've suffered a terrible lose with your husband dying in that fire this morning. She wants to comfort you."

Josephine pushed Willow off her lap. "I don't want her comfort. Look. She's gotten hair all over my clothes. Get her out of here."

Naya waved her hand. "You don't have to have her on your lap if you don't want to. But these cats are just part of the scenery. They've been here longer than I have—at least Nat has. He's the tabby. Did you see him upstairs in the station room?"

Josephine sniffed. "I can't say I did."

Naya arranged her papers on the table in front of her. "Nat has been here longer than anybody, even my partner Carl, who has been on this force the longest—of the humans, I mean." She laughed at her own joke.

Josephine scowled. "Can we get this over with? I have more important things to do."

"What could be more important that helping the police find your husband's killer?" Naya asked. "You should be the most interested in finding out who killed him."

Josephine shrugged. "You cops are all the same. You like to see crime and evil-doing around every corner. You're going to find out that fire was an accident."

"I don't think so," Naya countered. "We found the remains of cloth soaked in kerosene near the back oven. Someone set that fire deliberately to kill your husband."

Josephine cocked her head to one side. "Near the back oven, you say? You might as well know my husband Roy was the most irresponsible businessman you ever met when it comes to workplace safety. He was cited more than once by the health commission for unsafe gas lines leading to his ovens, and he stored chemicals inside the bakery that never should have been there. One spark could have ignited leaking gas and set off a chain reaction with the chemicals."

Naya looked up from her papers. "Now that is really helpful information, Josephine. I really appreciate you telling me that. We need that kind of information in this investigation."

"Now do you see what I mean?" Josephine replied. "No one killed him. He killed himself with his own negligence."

Naya went back to sorting her papers. "I understand. But we would still have to investigate. The arson investigator has to investigate any fire without a known cause. If we determine that Roy's death was not a homicide and the arson investigator determines that the fire wasn't arson, then we'll look at declaring his death accidental."

Josephine smacked her lips. "Don't you people realize the position this puts me in? I have to plan Roy's funeral, settle all his bank accounts, and lodge his death certificate with the county in order to get his will released. I can't do any of that until you cops declare the cause of death. Every hour of every day that passes costs me money."

"I understand this is hard on you," Naya replied. "You've suffered a terrible loss, and you want to put it behind you as quickly as possible. But the fire only happened this morning. You can't expect us to wrap up our investigation in one day."

"But it was an accident," Josephine insisted. "Can't you see that?"

Naya shook her head. "Even if we knew for certain that the fire was an accident, or the result of negligence on Roy's part, we would still have to follow our procedures and question everyone who knew anything about it."

Josephine crossed her arms over her chest. "Fine. Go ahead. What do you want to ask me?"

Naya smiled. "You weren't anywhere near the bakery this morning, were you?"

Josephine sat up so fast she almost shot out of her chair. "What are you trying to say? You're not accusing me of killing Roy, are you?"

"I never said anything of the kind," Naya replied. "I just asked a simple question. Where were you this morning?"

Josephine kept her eyes averted, but there

wasn't anything to look at in that room except the investigating officer across the table. "I was at home. I never went near the bakery."

Naya shuffled a few documents back and forth. "Do you know Jason Dempsey?"

"Of course, I know him," Jo shot back. "He's shift leader at the bakery."

"You mean, he *was* shift leader at the bakery," Naya corrected her. "He isn't anymore."

"What's that got to do with the price of eggs?" Josephine snapped.

"Jason is out of a job," Naya pointed out. "So is everyone else at the bakery, but Jason was there when the fire started."

"Are you looking at him as your prime suspect?" Josephine asked.

Naya shrugged. "Maybe. A lot of people are suspects in Roy's death, but Jason is the one with the most opportunity to start the fire."

"Then why isn't he locked up?" Josephine asked.

Naya set her papers aside and sighed. "It's like this. We have the same problem with Jason that we have with you. You're Roy's wife, so you could have all kinds of motives to get rid of him that we don't know about?"

"Like what?" Jo demanded. "What motive could I possibly have to kill my husband?"

"I don't know," Naya replied. "Maybe you couldn't wait to get your hands on the money in those bank accounts you want released. Like I said, you could have lots of motives."

"I didn't kill him," She maintained.

Naya got up and started pacing around the room. Josephine followed her with her eyes. "You could have a motive, but you had no opportunity. With Jason, we have the opposite problem. He had opportunity, but he has no motive—none that we know of, anyway."

"Well, there you go," Josephine remarked. "He had opportunity. You just have to figure out what his motive was, and you've got your killer."

"I'm afraid it's not as simple as that," Naya replied.

"What could be simpler?" Josephine asked.

"We have to prove that he killed Roy," Naya explained. "For that, we need evidence. We need evidence to substantiate his motive, and we need evidence to prove the method he used to start the fire without Roy's knowledge. It must have been hard for him to light it with Roy standing right there in the bakery with him."

Josephine turned away. "Not so hard."

Naya picked up a piece of paper. "The bakery schedule says they worked side by side on weekday mornings before the other employees came in. Roy would have met him at the door when he clocked in, and he would have had Jason in sight through his whole shift. How do you say Jason could go off into a corner and sabotage a gas line or tamper with chemicals?"

"I don't say anything," Josephine muttered.

"Did you have any dealings with Jason outside of the bakery?" Naya asked.

"I never had any dealings with him *in* the bakery," Josephine shot back. "I never had any dealings with him one way or the other. He was my husband's employee. I never said a word to him the entire time he worked for my husband."

Naya nodded. "Okay. I think we can wrap it up for today. We'll be in touch again when we get a little further along in our investigation."

"How long will that take?" Josephine asked.

Naya stood up and waved toward the door. "I really don't know. These cases can take a while to figure out. We'll let you know if we find out anything."

Josephine huffed and walked away. Carl met Naya at the door and they watched Josephine disappear up the stairs.

"Is Jason here?" Naya asked.

"He's waiting upstairs," Carl replied. "How's the grieving widow?"

"She wants us to hurry up our investigation," Naya told him, "and she doesn't believe it was murder. She says Roy neglected his safety obligations and the bakery burned down on its own."

"If it did," Carl shot back, "I'll eat my hat."

Naya snorted. "I'd like to see you try."

"What did she say about Jason?" Carl asked.

"She says she doesn't know him," Naya replied. "She says she never had anything to do with him."

"She probably didn't," Carl observed. "He worked for Roy, not her."

Naya gazed toward the empty stairs. "I don't know. Her husband hasn't even been dead twenty-four hours, and she's awfully anxious to get her hands on his bank accounts. She doesn't even want to wait until we determine the cause of death before she gets the death certificate filed and the will released."

"What's wrong with that?" Carl asked.

"Doesn't that make you suspicious?" Naya asked. "She and Jason could have something going on. They could have conspired to kill Roy to get his money."

Carl shrugged. "When my mother died two years ago, my father couldn't get all that paperwork sorted out fast enough. He wanted to get it done and put it behind him. Some people just deal with their grief that way.

CHAPTER 4

Carl pulled out Jason Dempsey's chair for him. Then he and Naya sat down opposite him. Willow crouched under the table. She didn't try to jump up into Jason's lap. This questioning of suspects was serious business, and she had to pay attention. She couldn't see Nat anywhere. He must be hiding somewhere in the shadows.

Carl pulled down the cuffs of his jacket sleeves. "So, Jason, we'll just go over a couple of the details we talked about this morning at the scene. Then you'll be free to go."

Jason shifted in his chair and looked around.

"I'm free to go now. You can't intimidate me. If I'm not under arrest, I can walk out of here at any time."

Naya looked up. "That's right, Jason. No one ever said otherwise. We're just here to ask a few questions about the fire."

"You can't fool me," Jason shot back. "I know the drill. I wouldn't be here right now if you didn't suspect me of starting the fire."

Carl cocked his head to one side. "If you know the drill, you must have a criminal record."

"Of course I have a criminal record," Jason snapped. "That was before I went to Boot Camp. Don't tell me you didn't look up my wrap sheet before you brought me in here. You wouldn't be much of a cop if you didn't."

Naya slid a manila folder across the table to Carl. Carl huffed and bent over it, but he didn't read it.

"Anyway, Jason," Naya went on, "let's go back to this morning when you were scheduled to work at the bakery."

"I already told you," Jason exclaimed. "I was nowhere near that bakery when it burned down. You have to believe me."

Naya held up the schedule. "You don't have to lie about it, Jason. You were scheduled to work this morning. Your girlfriend saw you leave home, and we have a witness who saw you park in the employee parking lot behind the bakery. We found the remains of the time clock with your imprint still on the tape. You clocked in right before the fire started."

"I clocked in," Jason told her, "but I wasn't in the bakery. I can prove it."

"How could you be anywhere else?" Carl asked. "If you clocked in, you were there."

"I clocked in," Jason explained, "but then I left. I was three blocks down the street when the building went up."

"What were you doing there?" Naya asked. "You were on the clock."

Jason fidgeted. "I'm telling you this in the strictest confidence, you understand. If I thought for a minute this information would get out, I would take it to my grave."

Carl stiffened. "If you have an alibi for the time of Roy Avino's death, you better tell us now. You wouldn't want us to think you had anything to do with it."

"You already think I had something to do with it," Jason returned. "I wouldn't be here now if you didn't think so. You think I started that fire, and that makes me a murderer."

"That's all the more reason to tell us your alibi," Naya pointed out. "I don't understand why you didn't tell us in the first place, unless you have something to hide."

"When I tell you the alibi," Jason replied, "you'll understand why I have something to hide. I was down the street behind the Nickel Alley Cafe with Josephine."

A tense silence fell over the room.

Jason nodded in answer to the detective's astonished stares. "Now do you understand? She made me swear on my mother's grave I wouldn't tell anyone, and I wouldn't if I wasn't facing a murder wrap for killing Roy."

Carl and Naya exchanged glances. "I just interviewed Josephine Avino in this same room," Naya told him. "She says she doesn't know you and never had anything to do with you."

"That's what she told everyone," Jason replied. "She never wanted anyone to find out about us."

Naya nodded. "I guess she didn't want Roy to find out."

Jason waved his hand. "She never cared about him. She originally started coming on to me to pay him back for fooling around on her."

Naya frowned. "She came onto you?"

Jason nodded. "I wouldn't make the moves on

the boss's wife. I wouldn't give her the time of day, but she wouldn't let up until I gave in. I've got a girlfriend to think about, you know."

Naya sighed, and Carl scratched his head. "I don't even want to know how you explain that one. So you were down behind the Nickel Alley Cafe with Josephine when the bakery went up in flames. How did you get out of your shift? Roy would have been standing right there."

"No, he wasn't," Jason countered. "After I clocked in, I searched the whole building for him, but he wasn't there. So I started making the dough for the cinnamon raisin bread. Then Josephine showed up at the back door and told me to come with her. I still had dough all over my hands."

"So off you went to the Nickel Alley Cafe," Carl added.

"Not to the Cafe," Jason corrected. "We were *behind* the Cafe."

"Of course you were," Naya replied. "We don't have to talk about what you two were doing there. But I think we can all agree your alibi is no good, Jason. Josephine says she never knew you. She says she never had anything to do with you in the bakery or out of it. She won't corroborate your story. You're right back where you started."

Jason stared at her. Then he slapped his thigh and let out a string of curses. "That little witch! Just wait until I get my hands on her."

Carl held up his hand. "You're not going anywhere near her."

"But she's leaving me in the lurch," Jason exclaimed. "She must have planned this whole thing. She must have knocked Roy out somewhere in the bakery and started the fire. Then she called me out to go with her while the place went up in flames. She must have planned to pin the murder on me all along."

"That's exactly why you're not going anywhere near her," Carl replied. "If she did plan it, then we all need to keep up the appearance of blaming you. You need to make yourself look as suspicious as possible so she won't know we're really moving in on her. She'll let her defenses down, and that's when we'll catch her."

Jason hesitated. Then he started laughing. "All right. I'll go along with it for now. Just as long as you both understand I didn't kill Roy."

Naya put out her hand to him, but she didn't touch him. "We both know that."

Jason leaned back in his chair with a sigh of relief. "Good."

"Now, then," Naya went on. "Just a couple more questions. You say Roy cheated on Josephine. Do you happen to know who he cheated with?"

"Everybody knows that," Jason replied. "He had a thing going with Marlena Rappaport for over five years. He even got his picture in the paper escorting her to the Metro Art Exhibition opening."

Carl rubbed his chin. "Marlena Rappaport, huh? Now that's punching above his weight."

"You're telling me," Jason returned. "Don't ask me how he bagged that bird, but he used to run off to her apartment in the middle of shifts all the time. She must have had him on speed-dial."

Naya chuckled. "I guess that's why Josephine

got you on speed-dial."

Jason made a disgusted face. "Josephine never had me on speed-dial."

"How often did she come to the back door of the bakery?" Naya asked.

Jason looked away. "Not often."

"Not often enough, you mean," Naya shot back. "Did she wait in her car across the street for Marlena to call up Roy, and then after he left, come to the back door to call you out to the Nickel Alley Cafe? Is that the way it worked?"

Jason dropped his voice to a husky whisper. "I don't know what you're talking about."

Naya pushed her chair back. "You can go now, Jason. You've been very helpful. If it makes you feel any better, I don't think you had anything to do with Roy's death. You can put your mind at ease on that."

Jason jumped up and grabbed her hand. He pumped it so hard he almost pulled it out of its socket. "Thanks a million, Detective. I knew I could count on you."

Naya laughed. "That's all right. I hope we can count on you if we need any more information for this case."

"Oh, absolutely, Detective," Jason exclaimed. "You can count on me. You can count on me for anything you need. Day or night, you call on me."

Naya smiled up at him. "Thank you. I will."

Jason tore out of the room. The next moment, you could hear the sound of his footfalls and drumming up the stairs. Carl gazed down at the stack of paperwork in front of him and shook his head. "What did you let him go so easy for? I had half a dozen more questions I wanted to ask him."

"Just wait a little while," Naya told him. "We'll bring him in for questioning again, and when we do, we'll have a lot more information to use against him. Right now, we have bigger fish to fry."

"You can't be thinking of Marlena Rappaport," Carl remarked. "She's got a national reputation as a film diva. She wouldn't stoop to killing a harmless baker."

"Who ever said Roy was harmless?" Naya asked. "Marlena could have some reason to want to get rid of him. Either way, even if she didn't kill him, we still have to question her."

"She didn't kill him," Carl insisted.

"What makes you so sure?" Naya asked.

"I know her," Carl replied.

"Personally?" Naya asked.

Carl shifted in his seat. "Well, no, not personally. But I've seen everything she's ever been in. She doesn't have any reason to get rid of Roy. Jason told you she let herself be photographed with him. She wouldn't have cared who knew they had something going. She wouldn't even have cared about Josephine finding out. She would probably be proud of the fact that she bagged a married man."

Naya turned away and headed for the door. "You might be right, but there's one more person we haven't thought about. There's one more person in this case who has a very distinct motive."

Carl frowned. "Who's that?"

"Jason's girlfriend," Naya replied. "Marlena might not care who found out about her and Roy, but Jason sure didn't want his girlfriend finding out about his relationship with Josephine."

Carl rifled through the papers. "Her name is Annika Neilsson. She lives in Cherry Tree Court."

"We'll question Marlena tomorrow morning," Naya decided. "Then we can start looking into Annika."

"But she would have no motive to kill Roy," Carl pointed out. "She probably didn't even know him."

"Maybe not," Naya replied. "But she could have had plenty of reason to frame Jason. If she found out about his fling with Josephine, she could have gotten mad and tried to pin the murder on him."

CHAPTER 5

Willow sat on Carl's desk and peered into the darkness. Nothing stirred in the deserted police station. Every now and then, a red light blinked on the smoke detector on the ceiling. Other than that, dead quiet filled the building.

Willow couldn't sit still. Her whiskers twitched, and her ears swiveled in every direction to catch the slightest noise. The tiniest tick of the clock sent her nerves jangling. She whispered into the darkness, "Are you there, Nat? Are you awake?"

For the first time in an eternity of waiting, a gruff voice answered her. "I'm awake."

Willow couldn't tell which direction the voice came from, but she jumped with a start and whirled around. "Where are you?"

A spot in the inky blackness caught her attention. A shadow moved in the gloom, but she couldn't make out any distinct shape. Only a semblance of movement convinced her Nat was somewhere over there.

Sure enough, his whiskers glistened in the moonlight. He blinked. Willow caught her breath. She kept a firm hold on herself to keep from racing toward him. She would have bowled him over and jumped on top of him with her fangs bared, but that was kitten play. Nat didn't play that way.

"What are we going to do?"

Nat sat down in the square of moonlight

streaming through the window. "You heard Naya. They're going to interview that Marlena woman in the morning. We have to get out and find some more information so we're ready."

"Ready for what?" Willow asked.

"Ready for the interview," he told her. "We're going to be there, and we need to get out and stir up more information before that happens."

"Get out—you mean, into the field?" Willow's heart beat faster.

"That's what I mean," Nat replied.

Willow couldn't hold herself back a second longer. She sprang off the desk and danced circles around Nat. She kept her composure just enough to avoid tackling him. "Oh, Nat! I can't wait. Just tell me what I have to do. Should I do anything to prepare? Should I groom myself first? Do I look okay the way I am now?"

"You look fine," he replied. "You don't have to do anything. You look a little too clean to go into the field as it is, but that's neither here nor there. You'll get dirty enough where we're going."

"Where are we going?" Willow asked.

Nat started toward the door. "You'll see." He slithered through the cat door and vanished into the night.

Willow raced after him, but when she got through the cat door, she couldn't see him anywhere. She paused and glanced around. Then she spotted Nat crossing the park across the street and dashed after him. She caught up with him next to the fountain and slowed to a walk at his side.

"I really appreciate you bringing me along," she panted. "I know I'm just learning detective work."

Nat shrugged, but he didn't look in her direction. He trained every sense into the wakening night. Willow watched him in awe. Every sound and smell brought him news of the wide world. He didn't get overwhelmed by the excitement of it all.

Nat was a real police cat. He'd seen it all before. He knew how to pace himself so every tin can with a piece of tuna fish sticking to it didn't send his heart fluttering. If only Willow could be like him.

She kept quiet until they crossed the railroad tracks. Then she just had to ask again. "Where are we going?"

"I have a couple of friends out here who can help us," Nat replied.

Willow almost stopped walking. "Friends? Who?"

Nat didn't answer. He scrambled over a chain link fence and dropped down on the other side. He walked up an alley, and Willow lost sight of him around a dumpster. She looked right and left. Should she follow him?

She didn't like where he was going, and she didn't want to go there after him. Her previous owner always told her to stay on the grass. Even Willow's own mother told her to stay clean and stay out of the dirt.

Willow looked up at the fence. Could she even climb it? Maybe she should head back to the station and leave the detective work to Nat. He was the expert. She was good at looking pretty and snuggling up to people.

All at once, Nat stuck his head out from behind the dumpster. "Are you coming or not?"

Willow wrinkled her nose up at the fence. "I don't think I can climb this."

Nat shrugged and turned away. "I guess you'll be left behind, then." He vanished.

Willow's heart sank. She couldn't let herself be left behind, not when she got all her hopes up of becoming a police cat like him. She took a few steps back and, with a deep breath, she took a run at the fence.

She never jumped over any fence before in her life. She had no idea how to go about it. When she judged she was close enough, she jumped blindly and put out her paws in a desperate hope of catching something.

One paw went through a hole between the wires, and she banged her nose on one of the links. She grunted in pain, but when her body hit the fence, instinct took over. Without thinking, she started clawing her way up. Her foot wound up in mid-air at every other step, but she couldn't do anything other than keep climbing.

At long last, she struggled over the top of the fence and the alley on the other side spread out before her. She caught her breath, but then she faced the greater challenge of getting down.

This time, she didn't give herself a chance to hesitate. If Nat could jump from that height without hurting himself, she could, too. He wouldn't expect her to do it if she couldn't do it safely. She took another deep breath and jumped.

She hit the ground on all four paws, and the

shock woke up some part of her cat soul she never knew she had. So this was how the other half lived. The cats who didn't have owners and police detectives putting food out for them and turning on the heater on winter days had to jump and climb and hunt for their living.

She stepped forward with a new confidence in her gait, but she stopped dead when she spotted Nat on the other side of the dumpster with two other cats. One was a dishwater grey Persian, but he wasn't a Persian like her. His face crunched up in a sour expression so he looked ready to bite anybody's head off that came too close. Dirt and rotten food caked his fur, and he didn't have any whiskers at all that Willow could see.

The other cat was a microscopic little scrap of a tortoise-shell Abyssinian. She looked like a kitten, except her head wasn't big enough compared to the rest of her body. What could make a cat so small, in spite of being a fully mature adult? She wasn't a miniature, either, only a tiny adult cat.

Willow almost lost heart again. Her mother always told her to stay away from alley cats. They didn't have the breeding of house cats, and they were smelly and dirty. That Persian certainly was, although the Abyssinian looked all right. Still, they were liable to do anything.

Nat sat down and looked around. "This is the new police station cat, Willow. I'm showing her around until she gets the hang of things."

The Persian scowled at Willow. She fidgeted. The Abyssinian bounced straight up in the air and landed on the very rim of the dumpster. Willow stared at her. How could any animal accomplish such a feat? Not even a cat could make that jump, and this cat didn't look big enough to jump out of a tea saucer, let alone up to the top of that dumpster. She didn't even crouch to spring first. She levitated straight off the ground like a puppet on a string.

The Abyssinian spoke down to Willow in a high-pitched squeak, and she spoke so fast Willow had to concentrate to catch every word. "You show 'em, girl. This town needs another police cat. You'll be the next wonder of the animal world before you know it."

Nat sniffed at a pile of something sticky on the pavement next to him and curled up his nose. "This is Chester, Willow. He looks terrible, but he's got his paw on the pulse of this town. Nothing happens in this town that he doesn't know about."

The Persian made a horrible face and turned

away. Willow never met a cat she wanted so much to have nothing to do with. But she couldn't back out now without disappointing Nat. He brought her here. He must have some reason for introducing her to these two oddities.

Nat flicked his ear at the Abyssinian. "This is Bella. Try to speak slowly, Bella, so Willow can understand you."

"I am speaking slowly," Bella squeaked.

Nat turned back to Willow. "I've known these two since I was a kitten. At least, I've known Chester since I was a kitten. I've known Bella since she was a kitten."

"How long ago was that?" Willow asked.

Bella let out a shriek that raised the hair on Willow's back on end. She hissed back at the tiny cat. Then she realized Bella was laughing.

"She's three years old," Nat told her. "She suffered terrible malnutrition in her first year, so she never grew any bigger than your average kitten. She's still like a kitten in a lot of other ways, but she's as sharp as a tack. She knows as much about everything in this town as Chester does, and that's saying something, considering he's almost four times her age. They can help us with the case."

Chester faced Nat. "So it's another case, is it? I suppose you're out to help Naya Wesley again, along with that dump of a partner of hers. Well, tell me the details and we'll see what we can come up with."

"It's about the Morningside Bakery fire," Nat replied.

"That just happened this morning," Bella observed.

"That's right," Nat replied, "Carl and Naya already have four suspects lined up."

"What are Carl and Naya doing investigating that fire?" Bella asked. "They're homicide detectives. Ross Bowen should be investigating. He's the arson investigator on the squad."

"The bakery owner was inside the building when it burned down," Willow replied. "Whoever set that fire killed him."

Chester crumpled his face up even more. "It was only a matter of time. Roy Avino deserved to die a nasty death. I knew someone would come after him eventually."

"What makes you say that?" Willow asked.

"He was a philandering clod," Chester growled. "He chased every woman in this town, and he didn't care who knew it. I suspect some jealous husband bumped him off."

Willow glanced at Nat. "Carl and Naya don't have any jealous husbands among their suspects."

Chester cocked his head. "They don't? Well, that just goes to show. I never was much of a police cat."

"You're better than a police cat," Nat remarked. "Why do you think we came to see you?"

"Why *did* you come to see us?" Chester asked.

"What do you know about Marlena Rappaport?" Nat asked.

"Everything," Chester replied.

Nat closed his eyes halfway. "Don't tell me you've seen all her films."

"I haven't seen any of them," Chester shot back. "But I've lived in the same town with her for over ten years. A cat can't help but hear things about her on the street."

"Tell me what you know about her," Nat urged.

"She's famous," Chester replied. "She's filthy rich, and she can get any man she snaps her fingers at."

"Like Roy Avino?" Willow asked.

"Just like Roy Avino," Chester replied. "If Marlena Rappaport blinks her fake eyelashes at a man, he's on his knees begging to serve her for life. Roy Avino was no different."

"I bet that left a lot of jealous wives around,"

Nat pointed out.

"Not as many as you might think," Chester replied. "Most of the wives of Marlena's men would be glad to have them after someone else for a change. Take Nick Porter, the owner of the Columba Street auto body shop. He did his dash with Marlena for over two years, but it wasn't until Marlena dumped him that his wife Trish divorced him and took half his assets in the bargain."

"Why did she do that?" Willow asked.

"Isn't it obvious?" Chester asked. "She didn't want him back. She didn't mind him running around with Marlena, making a fool out of himself in front of the whole town. At least Marlena kept him out of her hair. When he came crawling back to Trish with nothing but the shirt on his back, she kicked him in the teeth and sent him to live in the

Figure 8 Motel. He wasn't coming back to her for all the tea in China."

"That couldn't be happening between Josephine and Roy Avino," Willow reasoned. "Josephine got mad enough at Roy for taking up with Marlena that she hooked up with a penniless baker from the Morningside. She wouldn't have done that if she didn't want payback."

"Payback? Ha!" Chester grumbled under his breath. "Where have you been living, young lady—under a rock? Maybe she was waiting for years to go out on Roy. Maybe she had her eye on the baker from the beginning, and she only used Marlena as an excuse to get what she always wanted. We have no way of knowing if she was really angry and hurt. Maybe she was delighted."

Willow narrowed her eyes at him. "I may be

nothing but a glorified house cat, but you can't tell me a married woman would be glad to have her husband go after somebody else. People don't function that way."

Chester stared at her. Then he made an even more disgusting face and turned away. "You've got a lot to learn about human nature, little lady."

CHAPTER 6

"What can you tell us about the fire?" Nat asked.

Chester licked the front of his chest. "I can't tell you anything. I didn't even know it happened until you showed up here talking about it."

Bella jumped off the rim of the dumpster onto the lowest wrung of a fire escape hanging over her head. She scrambled up it onto a window ledge in the side of the building. She perched there and peered down at the cats on the ground below her.

Willow stared up at her in awe. If that tiny cat could jump and climb and balance that way, surely

Willow herself could do the same. She must have underestimated her own abilities. She would push herself harder from now on. She wouldn't rest until she became the best police cat ever.

"Don't listen to him, Nat," Bella piped. "That fire has been the talk of the town all day. Every cat in a seven-block radius came over to tell us about it, and they gave us all the details."

"Did they say anything about how the fire got started?" Nat asked.

"How could they know how the fire got started?" Chester asked. "I'm sure it got started in the usual way. The Morningside Bakery was located in an old building. The wiring must have given out and set the place on fire. It happens all the time."

"I'm afraid not," Nat returned. "Carl and Naya

found traces of cloth soaked in some kind of accelerant behind one of the ovens. They think it was used to set off the gas in the gas line. Josephine Avino says Roy was negligent and stored chemicals inside the bakery that shouldn't have been there. She thinks Roy's negligence started the fire."

Chester shrugged. "I don't know, but there's a very simple way to find out. A cat's nose is a lot stronger than anything the crime lab can come up with."

Bella took a flying leap off her window ledge and landed on all fours next to Willow. Willow jumped back in surprise. "Great!" Bella peeped. "We're going on a bear hunt!"

Willow gasped. "Bears!"

"That's just an expression," Bella told her. "It's

my way of saying we're going to do some hunting around."

"You mean, like going out into the field?" Willow asked.

Bella cocked her head to one side. "What field?"

Nat walked away down the alley. "We're already in the field, Willow. This is the field. Everything outside the police station is the field. What Bella means is that we're going to investigate the fire ourselves. We might find something Carl and Naya missed." Nat led the way, and Chester followed him. Willow scampered behind them.

Bella sprang up into the air again. This time, she didn't even touch the fire escape. She sailed straight to the window ledge. From there, she soared out over the alley and pounced onto the side of a brick. She didn't land on top of it. She landed on the side of the wall. Willow couldn't see a foothold anywhere on it, but Bella found some. She stuck to the side of the wall just long enough to make her next jump onto the back bumper of a car sitting up on blocks.

Every time Bella made one of her acrobatic leaps, Willow stopped to stare at her. "How do you do that?"

"Do what?" Bella chirped.

"That," Willow replied. "How do you jump like that from one place to the other? I never saw a cat do that."

"You can do it, too," Bella told her. "Any cat can do it."

"Really?" Willow asked. "Can Chester do it,

too?"

Bella paused. "Well, I've never seen him do it. But it's not difficult. You just have to try."

"Have you seen any other cats do it?" Willow asked.

"Well, no, now that you mention it," Bella replied. "But I'm sure there are lots of cats who can do it. I'm nothing special."

"You're not like any cat I've ever seen before," Willow told her. "Look at Nat and Chester up there. They walk along the ground. They don't fly through the air from one perilous brick to the next."

"You're the one who has an unusual life," Bella returned. "You live at the police station. That must be so exciting. I wish my life was half as interesting as yours."

"There's nothing interesting about the police station," Willow told her. "There's nothing to do but sit around and eat and sleep. Occasionally, you get to sit on someone's lap and they pet you. It's really boring."

"It can't be boring," Bella argued. "Look at you. You're out here investigating the Morningside fire. No other cat gets to do that."

"You're doing it right now," Willow pointed out, "and you're not a police station cat. I never would have thought twice about getting involved in police work if Nat hadn't told me I could and how to do it. He's the one you should admire, not me."

Bella gazed ahead at the two male cats walking side by side. "He really is an amazing cat. He's the smartest cat in town—except for Chester, of course."

"Is Chester your mate?" Willow asked.

Bella's tinkling laugh rang through the alley. "Chester? No, he's not my mate. I don't think Chester's had a mate in years." She laughed again.

"How did you end up living with him here in this...?" Willow trailed off.

"In this alley?" Bella asked. "It's okay. You can say it. There's nothing shameful about living in an alley."

Willow shook herself. "I'm sorry. It's just that my mother told me the most spine-chilling stories about alley cats. She said they were....Well, I won't tell you what she said."

"That's okay," Bella replied. "I know all about it. Chester told me certain housecats have a prejudice against alley cats. You think we're dirty and unscrupulous. I understand. But here you are, talking to one. It's not what you expected, is it?"

Willow cast a hesitant glance toward Chester. "I don't know. Chester certainly is the most unwashed cat I've ever laid eyes on."

Bella laughed again. "He hates washing. He's the only cat I've ever met that does. That's probably why he hasn't had a mate. I for one wouldn't go near him."

"How did you end up living in this alley?" Willow asked.

"I was born here," Bella replied. "I was born in that dumpster where I first met you. This is the first time I've ever left the alley."

Willow gasped. "Really? Why haven't you gone anywhere?"

"I was born in that dumpster," Bella explained, "and after the first week, my mother disappeared. I don't know what happened to her, but she never returned. I'm the only one of her five kittens who survived, and I had to learn quickly how to find food for myself."

"It must have been awful," Willow exclaimed.

Bella shrugged. "I learned that when you find a source of food, you hold onto it tooth and nail. If you have a steady supply of food, you stay near it and don't go wandering off where you might starve again. That's why I never left the alley."

"Does the alley have a good supply of food?" Willow asked.

Bella nodded. "That dumpster belongs to the Nickel Alley Cafe. They throw out all the scraps from the customers' plates. Chester and I have all the food we could want."

Willow cocked her head to one side. "The Nickel Alley Cafe?"

"That's what I said," Bella replied.

Willow stopped walking and turned toward Bella, but the tiny cat wouldn't stop bouncing from one place to another. Willow turned a complete circle trying to face her.

In the end, Bella landed on the lid of a metal trash can. The can teetered under her weight, and Bella crouched on it to gain her balance. Then she looked up at Willow. "What's the matter?"

"Where were you and Chester this morning, Bella?" Willow asked. "Where were you.....I'd say between the hours of seven and nine?"

Bella put her head to one side. "What?"

Willow took a step toward the trash can. "If you were in the alley this morning, you can give us some very important information about the fire?"

"How can I give you information about the fire?" Bella asked. "The bakery's three blocks away."

Willow dropped her voice, but her heart wouldn't stop pounding. "The baker, Jason Dempsey, says he wasn't in the bakery this morning when the fire started. He says he was here, behind the Nickel Alley Cafe, with Josephine Avino, the murder victim's wife."

Bella stared at her. Then she burst out laughing again. "You see what I mean? You sound like a police cat already." She started moving down the alley again.

Willow ran to catch up with her. "If you know something about this case, I sure wish you'd tell me. We can use all the help we can get to find out who killed Roy."

Bella sprang down to the ground and, for the first time, she stood perfectly still in front of Willow. "Josephine and Jason were in the alley. I saw them when I came out of the dumpster after breakfast. But Jason didn't stick around. He left... .I'd say about eight o'clock. You can ask Chester. He saw them, too."

Willow looked around. "Where are they?"

Bella trotted forward. "Don't worry. They went to investigate the fire."

"Where is that?" Willow asked.

"Right here." Bella turned a corner and

disappeared.

Willow ran after her and rounded the corner, but she froze in her tracks at what she saw. A big square of space between the buildings yawned wide and empty in the moonlight. Black charred remains of beams and sheetrock lay scattered over the ground, and piles of charcoal gleamed in the darkness. A few spikes of steel roof beams stuck up out of the ruins, but most of the concrete slab lay bare and blank before them.

Out of the darkness, a cat's sneeze brought Willow's attention to the far corner of the site. She shot forward and found Nat and Chester rummaging in a pile of broken glass and melted metal.

"Nat, Nat!" Willow panted. "Guess what? Chester and Bella live in that dumpster behind the

Nickel Alley Cafe. Bella says Josephine and Jason really were in the alley when the fire started. That means Jason's alibi is solid."

Nat pulled his head out from under a charred two-by-four. "I'm glad to hear you're keeping your wits about you, Willow, but I already discussed the situation with Chester. He saw Josephine and Jason in the alley this morning, too."

"It looks like Naya was right," Nat replied. "If Jason's alibi is solid, then he's innocent and someone framed him for this murder. Too many of the other suspects have a motive to undermine him and pin Roy's death on him."

"How can you be certain Naya believes that?" Willow asked. "I understood from Carl's remarks that she only told Jason she thought he was innocent."

Nat sneezed again and bent over the burned remains of the bakery. "I don't think so. She might not have completely ruled him out, but he didn't kill Roy. He had no motive, and now we've got corroboration of his alibi. Meanwhile, we have three other people with motives to frame him."

"Three?" Willow asked. "I can only think of two— Josephine and Annika Neilsson."

"There's Marlena," Nat replied.

"What motive could she possibly have to frame Jason?" Willow asked. "She didn't even know him."

"If she had a reason to kill Roy," Nat replied, "she would want someone to frame, wouldn't she?"

"She had no reason to kill Roy," Willow argued.

"None that we know of," Nat corrected her. "Maybe she didn't care who knew they were messing around with each other, but she could have had another reason. We'll find that out tomorrow when Carl and Naya go to interview her."

CHAPTER 7

Nat and Chester stuck their noses farther into the piles of charcoal and wooden fragments. Chester came out more soiled and grimy than when he went in. Willow barely recognized him. He didn't even look like a cat anymore. He reminded her of some kind of reptile she saw on *Animal Planet*. "What are you looking for?"

Nat sat back and brushed the soot off his whiskers. "I had occasion to go into the Morningside Bakery once. This is the corner where the ovens were hooked up to the gas lines. This would be the corner where the crime lab found the accelerant that started the fire."

"How did you manage to get inside the bakery?" Willow asked.

Nat shrugged and turned away. "Roy left the back door open on hot summer afternoons. The smell was irresistible. I went in and stole one of the fresh chocolate chip cookies. I ran off with it while Roy was on the phone. He never even knew I was there."

Chester chuckled to himself. "That's just like you, Nat. You're a terror."

Willow shook her head in wonder. "I wish I had the guts to do something like that."

Nat started cleaning his face. "Everybody's got to start somewhere. You were a housecat until you came to the police station. I was born wild, so these things come naturally to me. You'll get the hang of it, but you have to start practicing your craft."

Willow nodded. "I'm beginning to understand that."

Bella touched a charred piece of metal with her paw. "So what did you find? Did you detect any accelerant among the remains of the bakery equipment?"

"As I told you," Nat replied, "a cat's nose is several hundred times more sensitive than any detection method the crime lab uses. There are traces of several chemicals in this corner. One of them is paint stripper, and another is toluene with a trace of hydrocarbon propellent. That kind of product comes in a spray can. Roy would have used to clean the chrome on his BMW motorcycle."

"Then Josephine was right," Willow remarked. "Roy kept chemicals in the bakery, and that's what set off the fire."

"Not so fast," Chester added. "We also detected a variety of jet fuel with an admixture of stabilizer to keep it in a liquid state. The only place you find that particular combination of fuels is in certain proprietary blends of camping stove cartridges."

Willow blinked. She didn't understand half the big words the tom cats used. "Camping stoves? How did that wind up in the bakery?"

Chester sneezed again, but he made no effort to wash the black grime off his face and body. He must have enjoyed making a startling impression. "That's precisely the point, my dear. It wouldn't have wound up in the bakery unless someone put it there. Roy never went camping in his life, and neither did Josephine."

"Someone started that fire by planting camping fuel in the bakery," Nat added. "The question is, who had an interest in camping?"

"Jason," Chester replied.

Nat's head shot up, and Willow whirled around to face him. "He did?"

Chester snorted. "You police cats don't have your ears to the ground like we do. You need an alley cat to tell you these things. Jason went camping almost every weekend. He would have had those cartridges."

"Tell the whole story, Chester," Bella chided. "Jason wasn't the only one who went camping. He took his girlfriend Annika with him when he went. She had access to those fuel cartridges, too."

"That's another reason to believe she had something to do with the murder," Nat remarked. "She could have started the fire to cast the blame back on Jason."

Willow shook her head. "Wait a minute. Bella says Jason left the alley about eight o'clock. What if he went back to the bakery and started the fire? He could be the one trying to frame Annika."

Nat licked his now-clean lips. "When you've been in this business as long as I have, you develop a sense of who's innocent and who isn't. I have a feeling about Jason Dempsey, and he didn't kill Roy."

"Not so fast, my friend," Chester grumbled. "You may be resident police cat around here, but stand aside for the superior skills of the alley cat. Over here, you'll find the trace of another chemical

I believe sheds a new light on this case."

The other cats ran to the spot, and Chester flipped over a shard of twisted metal with his paw. "What is it?"

"It looks like a soda can," Willow remarked.

"It's the last fragment of the fuel cartridge," Chester told them. "It must have exploded when the fire hit it. You can smell the fuel on it."

"But that doesn't tell us anything," Nat pointed out. "We already know the killer started the fire with a fuel cartridge."

"But there's another smell on the cartridge, too," Chester replied. "Come have a whiff."

Willow put her nose against the metal and took a deep sniff. "It smells like alcohol."

"That smell, my dear little house cat," Chester intoned, "is what human beings call perfume. It's a chemical they use to make themselves smell a certain way. It's like spray, but it's artificial. It's designed to disguise how they really smell."

Willow frowned. "But what's the point of that? Their natural smells send signals back and forth so they can find suitable mates. Why would they want to disguise that?"

"My point exactly," Chester growled. "They use these smells to make each other think they're more suitable than they really are. Sometimes the strategy works, but more often than not, it fails. Humans are much more attracted to their mates' natural smells than even they realize or would be willing to admit."

"What my esteemed colleague of the alley hasn't

told you, though," Nat countered, "is that perfume is most often used by women, which would confirm my theory that Annika planted the camping fuel to frame Jason."

"What my esteemed colleague of the police department doesn't realize," Chester shot back, "is that this is a special kind of perfume known in the human world as cologne. It is used by men."

Willow and Bella looked back and forth between the two cats.

"Roy could have been wearing that cologne," Nat argued.

Chester drew himself up. "Are you telling me Roy Avino handled the fuel cartridge that took his life?"

"If Josephine is right," Willow added, "he could

have left the cartridge here and left his cologne on it."

"But," Chester pointed out, "we already determined that Roy didn't go camping. I can also personally testify that he never wore cologne. He was a sloven, and you can take my word that the term is a very generous one."

Bella tittered. "Look who's talking."

Chester ignored her. "Jason, on the other hand, always went about the town drenched in cologne of this variety. He fancied himself some kind of dandy. I can only imagine his fling with his boss's wife colored his imagination."

"That still doesn't rule out the possibility that Annika planted the cartridge to frame Jason," Nat pointed out. "She could have selected a cartridge that had Jason's cologne on it, or she could have put his cologne on it herself to make it look like he put the cartridge in the bakery."

Willow blinked. "This Annika would have to be pretty devious to plan something like that. I wonder what she's like."

"You won't have to wonder," Nat told her. "We're going to visit her tomorrow, right after we interview Marlena Rappaport."

"We?" Willow asked. "We interview Marlena?"

Nat shrugged and turned away. "You know what I mean."

Chester waved his paw the other way. "One more thing. Over here, we have another distinct chemical smell."

"What is it?" Willow asked.

"It belongs to a certain class of explosives known as blasting caps," Chester told her. "I would say the killer planted them close to the fuel cartridge to set it off. I haven't seen the cartridge in its whole state, so maybe it had a safety device that prevented it from igniting on its own. The killer needed something to ignite it."

Nat spun around. "But who would have access to that?"

Chester poked the debris with his nose. "These blasting caps are military grade. They contain traces of ignition fuels found only in the military. Whoever used them had a military background."

"That should help us narrow down the list of suspects," Willow remarked. "Which of them had a military background, Nat?"

Chester turned to Nat. "Yes, Nat. Please tell us which of the suspects had a military background."

Nat kept walking. "Let's go, Willow. We're done here for tonight."

Chester chuckled, and he and the other cats followed Nat to the edge of the crime scene. They walked under the yellow police cordon tape warning everybody to stay out. The cats stopped, and Willow looked back. "We didn't find the clues to solve the case."

"The important thing is to collect all the pieces of the puzzle," Nat told her. "Only after you have them all do you start fitting them together to make a complete picture of what happened."

Willow turned to Bella. "What will you two do for the rest of the night?"

"I'm meeting friends near the movie theater," Bella replied. "I'm not sure, but I think Chester is meeting the other toms for choir practice on the roof of the apartment building at the end of the alley. They have twenty toms who get together to test their voices against each other."

Willow giggled. "I'll bet the people in the apartment building love that."

"They do," Bella told her. "They always come to their windows to listen, and they even shout encouragement. Some even throw presents."

"I wish we didn't have to go so soon," Willow exclaimed. "We only just met, and I have so many things I want to ask you about."

Bella laughed. "I bet you never thought you'd want to spend any time with an alley cat."

Willow blushed. "You're right. You've completely changed my opinion. I'm sorry for judging you the way I did."

"Never mind," Bella replied. "We can be friends now. And don't worry about leaving. If you want to talk again, you know where to find me."

Willow waved her tail in the air. "Thanks. It sure helps to know I have someone out in the field I can count on."

Nat called to her over his shoulder. "Come on, let's get going."

CHAPTER 8

Willow followed Nat, and Chester and Bella disappeared into their alley. Willow cast one last look at them before they vanished into the shadows. "They really are an amazing pair."

"No police cat could solve a case without them," Nat agreed. "There's an old saying. 'It's not what you know, it's who you know.' They've helped me a dozen times or more. They can tell you things you would never be able to figure out on your own."

"You mean like finding that cologne?" Willow asked.

Nat made a face. "I don't think that cologne

contributed much to the case, but Chester did, and I defer to his expertise. We can add it to our store of information about the suspects, but it does seem to point very strongly to Jason and Annika. Those two have the highest likelihood, in my opinion, of being the killers."

"Maybe they did it together," Willow suggested.

Nat cast her a sidelong glance. "I wouldn't be surprised. I also wouldn't be surprised if Josephine and Jason did it together. When people cheat on their spouses, they don't have very far to go before they decide to rid themselves of their old partners altogether. The temptation to murder can become overwhelming."

He turned a corner and climbed a set of concrete stairs to the roof of the Motel building. "Look at that," Willow remarked. "I didn't know we'd been out so long, but the sky is getting light. We better get back to the station to meet up with Carl and Naya. We don't want to miss out on Marlena's interview."

"We are not going back to the station," Nat informed her.

"What?" she cried. "Why not? Did you decide not to interview Marlena after all."

"We're going to interview her," Nat told her. "We just won't bother to go back to the station first."

Willow blinked. "I don't understand you."

"Do you see that building over there?" Nat asked. "That's the Montague Estates Apartments. I know it well, because the Nelson Toms Choir used to meet there every second Sunday of the month."

"Is that the group Chester belongs to?" Willow asked.

"Yes, and I used to belong to it, too," he told her. "That was before I joined the Highland Golf Course Toms Choir. But what I really wanted to tell you is that Marlena lives at the Montague Estates Apartments. We can get there much faster from here. Going back to the station would only waste our time, and we would probably both fall asleep there and miss the interview."

"But we have hours to wait before Carl and Naya come to interview Marlena," Willow pointed out. "We could have a nap in the meantime and still get out in time for the interview."

Nat shook his head. "Even if we did wake up in time to leave the station, we would attract too much attention leaving at the same time Carl and Naya did. Our best bet it to hunker down somewhere near Marlena's apartment so we're on the spot when they show up. As it happens, I know the perfect spot."

"Where?" Willow asked.

Nat trotted across the street toward the building. "Follow me."

Willow joined him.

"Do you see that alley next to the building?" Nat Asked.

Willow caught her breath. "There's a cat."

"That's Thorndale Alley," Nat told her. "It's full of cats. It's one of the strongest alleys in town. If you ever need alley cats and can't find Chester and Bella to help you, call on the Thorndales. They're a very powerful family, and they can do pretty much whatever they have to do. They'll be good cats for you to get to know."

Willow hesitated. "I don't think I want to go in there."

"We're not going in there," Nat told her, "not right now, anyway. I just want you to know about it. There's another alley on the other side of the building. That's Stevenson Alley, and it's full of cats, too."

"Are they friends with Thorndale Alley?" Willow asked.

"No," Nat snapped. "Not by a mile. They hate each other, and it's taken years of work by cats like Chester and Rondo James to stop them warring in the streets."

"Who's Rondo James?" Willow asked.

"He's another very old and very powerful alley cat," Nat told her. "He and Chester negotiated a partial truce between Stevenson and Thorndale, just to keep the bloodshed to a minimum, but the two families still don't like each other. They stick to their own alleys, or they would kill each other on sight."

Willow shuddered. "I think we should go back to the station."

"Keep your shorts on," Nat growled. "You are not in any danger from either one of them, and you might need them one day. This neighborhood is crawling with cats. That will come in handy for us this morning."

He found an iron staircase running up the side of the building, and he and Willow climbed up a series of fire escapes to a balcony.

"This is Marlena's apartment," Nat told her. "We can settle down here and take a nap before Carl and Naya get here. Marlena sees cats on her balcony all the time, so she won't suspect us of anything. In fact, she might even give us something to eat."

Willow tried to peer through the window, but the curtains were shut. "How will we hear the interview?"

"Once the sun comes up and the heat rises," Nat explained, "Marlena will open the window. We'll be able to hear every word they say. If that doesn't work, we can claw at the window and beg for food."

"Does that work?" Willow asked.

"All the time," Nat replied. "The instant she opens the door, you run inside like you own the place and start meowing as loud as you can. You pace back and forth in front of the refrigerator until she gets the idea. Nine times out of ten, she'll feed you right there in the kitchen. People don't want to walk all the way back out to the balcony to feed you. We'll be in the apartment while Carl and Naya question her."

"That sounds like a perfect plan," Willow exclaimed. "You're a genius, Nat."

"Hardly," he muttered. "Any cat could tell you the same thing. All you have to do to get a human being to do what you want is pretend to be a tame house cat. Humans are used to that. They like feeding house cats and having them in their houses."

Willow sat down in the corner of the balcony and narrowed her eyelids. "This is nice. I could get comfortable here."

"Take a nap, but don't get comfortable," Nat ordered. "After Carl and Naya interview Marlena, we'll go see what we can find out about Annika. You'll need all your resources for that. We don't know what we'll find."

Willow curled up in a ball in the corner and closed her eyes. She didn't realize how much her night in the field exhausted her. She wasn't used to all the excitement, and the adventure wasn't over yet. In an instant, she fell asleep.

Nat sat to one side and gazed at her for a while. He didn't usually go for those immaculate house cats, but he couldn't deny his attachment to Willow. Her plucky determination to master the art and skill of police work endeared her to him beyond anything he ever would have expected.

Pride and paternal protection filled his being when he introduced her to his alley cat friends.

She snoozed away, and her delicate fur rippled when she breathed. He could sit up all morning and watch her sleep, but he needed to rest himself. He watched her for another ten minutes. Then he sighed and curled up next to her. She stirred in her sleep and sank back into the depths of slumber. Nat closed his eyes and dropped off, too.

Two hours passed, and the sun rose against the side of the apartment building. The heat woke up Nat, but Willow slept on. In the end, he nudged her with his paw. She stirred, but she didn't open her eyes. "Go away."

Nat sighed. "Wake up, Willow. It's almost ten o'clock."

Willow blinked and sat up. She looked around and yawned. "Where are we?"

"Don't you remember?" he asked. "We're on Marlena Rappaport's balcony, and Carl and Naya just showed up to interview her."

Willow looked around again. "How can you tell?"

Nat peered through the apartment window. "They're in there right now. If you look, you'll see them."

CHAPTER 9

A stately woman with straight blonde hair carried her dewy glass across the main room of the apartment and slid open the window. "I can't stand when it gets so hot in here. I need air."

Carl and Naya exchanged a grin. The lace curtains hid Nat and Willow on the balcony right outside the window, so they didn't see their own station cats listening to their interview.

"We just want to ask you a few questions, Marlena," Naya began. "You may have heard that Roy Avino was killed yesterday morning."

Marlena waved her hand. "I don't appreciate

you calling me by my first name, Detective. You can call me Miss Rappaport until we're on a first name basis."

"We could be on a first name basis now, if you like," Naya replied. "I don't mind you calling me Naya."

"I don't think so," Marlena growled.

Naya shrugged. "That's okay. We all know you had a relationship with Roy, so that gives you a motive to kill him."

"Everybody had a motive to kill Roy," Marlena told her. "That guy had more enemies than whiskers."

Carl snorted. "That's a good one."

Marlena turned a withering stare at him. "I'm not joking. Anybody could tell you Roy Avino was going to wind up at the bottom of the harbor wearing concrete sneakers."

Naya bit her lip to stop herself from smiling. "That's interesting, but Roy didn't drown wearing concrete sneakers. Someone burned down his bakery with him inside it."

Marlena narrowed her eyes. "Then it must have been started by someone who worked there."

Carl and Naya looked at each other. "What makes you say that?"

"Isn't it obvious?" Marlena asked. "Whoever lit the fire had to get into the bakery somehow. How could they do that if they didn't work there?"

Carl shrugged. "Good point."

"Did you know anyone who worked there?" Naya asked.

Marlena rubbed the drops of condensation on her glass. "Only Roy. I don't mix with plebeians."

"We're plebeians.," Naya pointed out.

"I wouldn't mix with you, either, Detective," Marlena replied.

"Roy was a plebeian," Naya went on. "You definitely mixed with him. You even let the local paper print a picture of the two of you together at the Metro opening."

Marlena waved her bejeweled hand. "That was nothing, and Roy was nothing. I'm sure the world is a much better place without him."

"That's the kind of thing I would expect to hear from the person who killed him," Naya told her.

Marlena shrugged. "I didn't kill him. I wouldn't stoop so low. If I wanted Roy dead, I could have taken any number of opportunities over the years to bump him off. I know enough heavyweights in organized crime that you detectives wouldn't come knocking on my door to find out who killed him. You would never even know he'd been murdered. Whoever got rid of Roy did a very amateurish job, if you ask me."

"Where were you yesterday morning, Marlena?" Naya asked. "Where were you between the hours of seven and nine?"

Marlena fixed Naya with an icy glare, but she didn't bother to correct her for calling her by her first name. "I was in a meeting with my agent. He can vouch for me."

Naya's eyebrows went up. "You were in a meeting at seven o'clock in the morning? I find that hard to believe."

"If you don't want to take my word for it," Marlena replied, "you can check with his secretary. His building has security cameras over the doors and in the elevators and in all the hallways. You can check them for yourself, and you'll see that I was with him all morning."

Nat turned away from the window and whispered to Willow. "Come on. Let's get out of here."

"But the interview isn't over," Willow pointed out.

Nat jumped onto the fire escape and started picking his way down to the ground. "The interview doesn't matter anymore. Marlena has an ironclad alibi. We don't have to waste any more time on her."

Willow's heart pattered when she got to the top of the fire escape. The ground reeled far below her. How could she ever climb all the way down without falling? Then she remembered Bella. The tiny Abyssinian would probably jump from the balcony all the way down to the ground in one spring without scratching her little toenails.

Willow plucked up her courage and set off down the fire escape after Nat. "But you don't really believe Marlena's story about being in a meeting with her agent. That must have been a lie."

Nat sighed. "You're a young cat, Willow, and you don't know much about what goes on in this town. Marlena's agent is Hanford Laghlan. He's a known lady's man, and he's had a thing going with Marlena for years. He's also extremely rich and lives in one of the most expensive apartment buildings in the city."

Willow stopped and stared at him. "Do you mean she wasn't really in a meeting with him at seven o'clock in the morning?"

Nat chuckled. "Let's just say it was a meeting, but it wasn't a business meeting. What Marlena said about his building having security cameras everywhere is true. She wouldn't use Hanford Laghlan as an alibi if she wasn't sure the cameras would corroborate her story. I'm afraid her alibi is a lot more water tight than Jason's."

"So what are we going to do next?" Willow asked. "How can we find out if Jason was in the alley with Josephine at the time of Roy's murder? Chester and Bella said he left at eight. Maybe he went back to the bakery and lit the fire."

Nat stopped on the last fire escape platform. "We'll go interview Annika Neilsson right now."

"How will we interview her?" Willow asked. "Are Carl and Naya going there after they finish with Marlena?"

"No." Nat looked down at the apartment building parking lot. "Look. There they go. They're heading back to the station. It must be getting close to lunch time. Maybe they'll interview Annika this afternoon. They must have realized Marlena's alibi was too good for her to be the killer. I knew she didn't kill Roy. She has no motive and a heck of a lot to lose if she got caught."

"Oh, look at that, Nat!" Willow exclaimed.

The two cats sat still and watched Marlena Rappaport come out of the building. She paused to look both ways, but when she saw the parking lot empty, she hurried out and got into a lime green Porsche coop. The engine roared, and she screeched out of the parking lot.

"Where is she going?" Willow asked.

"I don't know," Nat replied, "but we can't follow her. Let's get over to Annika's house and see what we can find out."

He jumped to the ground, and Willow dropped down next to him. The thrill of success rippled through her body when she landed on all four feet with a satisfying spring. She trotted after Nat with a hop and a skip.

Nat glanced over at her. "You're sure enjoying yourself."

"You were right," she replied. "Getting out into

the field and investigating cases is much more interesting than sitting around the station all the time. And that nap this morning was just what the doctor ordered."

"We are not finished yet," he told her. "We've got the rest of the day, and the rest of the case to solve."

They darted down the street. They stopped in the shadows of buildings and garbage cans to look around, but no one noticed them. Willow followed Nat's lead, and after a while, they left the congested city center for the outlying residential neighborhoods.

"I recognize this place," Willow remarked. "I think I used to live here before I came to the police station."

"That's not very likely," Nat returned. "There are dozens of these neighborhoods all over town, and they all look exactly the same. You could have come from any of them."

Willow fell silent, but the farther they traveled, the faster her heart beat. "I definitely think I recognize this place. Look at that playground over there with all the kids in it. I've seen that before."

"You've seen it on every street corner," Nat shot back. "Come on. Stop lagging. The case won't solve itself."

Willow gazed at the children swinging on the swings and spinning around on the monkey bars. Their delighted laughter and shouting sent a chill up her spine. That sound called to her from out of her past. Could she find the place she lived before Naya brought her to the police station? Could she find her way back home to the people who cared for her?

Then she remembered her desire to become a police cat like Nat. She couldn't go home again if she wanted to be one. She had to learn to read suspects, climb fire escapes and dig for clues in crime scenes. Her past life was gone forever.

But the voices of the children wouldn't let her go. She took a step toward the playground. She had to find out what about them bewitched her heart and mind.

She cast a glance at Nat, but he was already halfway down the block. If he noticed her stray, he didn't show it. Willow didn't let herself hesitate a second longer. She ran after Nat and raced him around the corner where she couldn't hear the children anymore.

"There it is," Nat told he.

"What?" she asked.

He pointed his nose toward a little brick cottage behind a thick hedge. "That's Annika Neilsson's house. That's where she lived with Jason for the last year and a half."

Willow took a step forward. "Great. Let's go."

"Not so fast. Take a look over there." He pointed his nose the other way.

A lime green Porsche coop sat parked down the block and around the corner. Willow hadn't noticed it between two trees. "What's that doing here?"

"Good question," Nat growled. "But we can't just walk in the front door like I planned. We'll have to go around the back way."

"But didn't you say nobody notices a cat listening to their conversations?" Willow asked. "They wouldn't care if we did walk in the front door."

Nat headed toward the hedge. "It's better to be safe than sorry."

He ducked under the hedge, but he didn't come out again. Willow waited for him, but when he didn't reappear, she tiptoed toward the hedge. "Nat? Are you there?"

No sound came from the wall of vegetation. Willow crouched down. She pushed her head under the lowest bushy branch and came face to face with Nat. "What are you doing under there?"

"Don't say anything," he whispered. "Just do exactly as I do."

"But there's no danger here," she pointed out. "No one knows us here."

He hissed at her and slithered away through the dirt. Willow hated to get her fur dirty, but she didn't see how she had much choice but to follow him.

The hedge ran up the side of the house and around the back yard. How did Nat know where to stay under the hedge to keep hidden and where to come out when he wanted to dart up to the back door? Willow shouldn't have wondered that he knew every detail of every inch of the city. He must have been doing this detective work since long before she was born.

He squeezed out from under the hedge and peered around. Then he ran in a line straight for the open back door. Willow hesitated a moment longer. Nat couldn't be wrong, and even if he was, what could possibly go wrong? If the owners found a couple of stray cats in their house, they might yell and wave their arms until the cats ran away. They couldn't exactly call the police, could they?

CHAPTER 10

Willow ran to Nat's side at the back door, and they both froze with every hair on high alert. Then Nat ventured onto the cold linoleum of the kitchen floor. Not a sound echoed through the house. Willow crept after him, but something caught her attention that distracted her.

She wrinkled her nose toward the corner by the refrigerator. A cat food smell clung to the base board and the crack where the linoleum met the wall. Saliva filled her mouth. A memory of food flooded her mind, so she almost forgot to follow Nat into the hall.

Nat crouched in the middle of the hall and listened. Human voices came from one of the rooms. Willow trotted to his side, but another cluster of smells assaulted her brain from the bathroom. Mixed in with the stench of disinfectant and shower gel, rose the combination of human bodies, and not just any human bodies. She knew these people. She was never more certain of anything in her life.

A shout brought her attention back to the business at hand. "How many times do I have to tell you? I can't get access to the money until the police finish their investigation. I've tried, but they have procedures to follow."

Another female voice answered the first, and Willow couldn't mistake it for anyone other than Marlena Rappaport. "This isn't what we planned. I should have known better than to trust you."

"You can rant and rave all you want. That's not going to get you your money any faster." Willow recognized the first voice as belonging to Josephine Avino. "We planned everything down to the smallest detail, but we didn't plan on waiting around to get our pay-off. You'll just have to put your cruise to French Polynesia on hold, just like the rest of us."

A third voice joined the conversation. Willow recognized that voice, too, but she couldn't quite place it. "So what are we going to do?"

"There's nothing we can do but wait," Josephine replied. "The police interviewed me and Marlena. Now it's your turn, Annika." So the third voice belonged to Annika Neilsson.

"What are they going to interview me for?" Annika asked. "I didn't even know Roy, and I didn't have any reason to kill him."

"You had a reason to frame Jason for the murder," Josephine replied. "You have to admit, Annika, in the eyes of the police, you had just as much to gain by getting rid of Roy as Marlena and I did."

"I had a lot more reason to do it than either of you," Annika shot back. "and I could end up being the one who goes down in all of this. If I don't get my share of the bank accounts, I could lose my house. I could lose everything."

"Don't sing me that song of heartbreak," Marlena snapped. "Everybody thinks because I'm some kind of film star that I'm rolling in loot. It isn't true. I haven't worked on a film in ten years, and no one signs me for endorsements anymore. I've been living on my credit cards for over a decade."

"Who's fault is that?" Annika returned. "So you squandered your fortune. Cry me a river. You've never had to do a day's work in your life."

"Get over it, Annika," Josephine grumbled. "Jason's been supporting you with his bakery wages ever since you two first moved in together. Why do you think he started looking for a woman with some motivation? If you're going to lose your house, you could always go out and get a job of your own. You don't have to sit here complaining about it."

"Don't start in on me," Annika shouted back. "You have nothing to blame me for. You milked Roy for every penny you could get. Then he wised up to the fact that you only cared about his money, and he took away your ATM card. That's when you came up with this idea to kill him for the last of his cash. Jason may have supported me, but at least I wasn't spending his money on high-priced shoes."

Marlena laughed, but her laugh sounded like glass breaking under a car tire. "Girls, girls, girls. We don't have to fight amongst ourselves. We're all in the same boat."

"That's easy for you to say," Annika countered. "I'm the one who put that fuel cartridge in the bakery. If those police detectives suspect me of anything, I'm sunk and you two will ride off into the sunset with Roy's money. I'll bet you planned it that way from the very beginning."

"You may have put the cartridge there," Josephine told her, "but Marlena and I are just as culpable of murder as you are. The murder never would have succeeded without each of us playing our parts. I was the one who told Roy I needed to speak with Jason and got him out of the bakery so that you could sneak in the back.

"If I hadn't kept Roy occupied on the phone," Marlena added, "you wouldn't have been able to put the cartridge behind the oven without getting caught."

"So you see," Josephine went on, "we're all in this together."

"Still," Annika argued. "You've both faced the interrogation chamber with perfectly good alibis. I still have to go through the questioning without one."

"I don't have an alibi," Josephine pointed out. "I had to tell those cops I didn't know anything about Jason Dempsey and I wasn't with him when the fire started. Leaving him without an alibi left me without an alibi."

"What about you, Marlena?" Annika asked. "You can't claim to be in the same boat with the rest of us. You're not a suspect for this murder."

Marlena considered the matter. "I admit I do have the best alibi of the three of us. I planned it that way. I didn't want to live in mortal fear of the day some flatfoot showed up on my door. I did my part to bump off Roy Avino from the safety of a maximum security apartment. The security cameras can prove I was nowhere near the bakery when it caught fire. If you girls had any imagination, you would have come up with alibis of your own."

"I couldn't exactly come up with an alibi, could I?" Annika replied. "Someone had to do the dirty work of going into the bakery."

Something moved in the room from which the voices came, and footsteps approached the door. Willow crouched in readiness to flee, but something she couldn't understand made her hesitate one last time. Was it fear, or something familiar?

Nat didn't stick around to find out what would happen next. He tore sideways into another bedroom, skated across the hardwood floor, and flew into the open window. He landed on the windowsill and looked back to wait for Willow.

Even when she heard the footsteps coming toward her, she couldn't make herself run until the last possible moment. There was still one element missing to this mystery, and what struck her as so familiar?

Annika shoved the door open and burst out of the room. She stood all of six foot three inches, and her lithe body stretched almost up to the ceiling. Her curly blonde hair hung almost to her waist. She strode down the hall heading for the kitchen or the bathroom.

Willow froze with every muscle taut to spring, but when her eye fell on Annika's face, the puzzle pieces settled into place. She no longer thought about running away. She no longer thought about being a police cat. She no longer thought about anything at all. Her mind went blank.

Annika's mouth fell open. "There's a cat in here. It looks like my old cat." She put out her hand. "Here, Snowy. Come here, pretty girl."

Willow stared at her. Then, out of the depths of her soul, she meowed.

Nat called to her from the window in that intense whisper that forced her to look in his direction. "Are you coming, Willow?"

As soon as she looked away from Annika's face, the spell shattered. She ran for all she was worth, down the hall, past the pictures and the medals hanging in frames, past the gilded citations and the smelly bathroom. She didn't bother to stop on the windowsill. In one flying leap, she cleared the window ledge and landed on the concrete outside.

Every fiber knew what to do when she hit the ground. She rocketed forward and dove under the hedge. She didn't stop running until the prickly darkness closed around her and blocked out the memory of everything she just saw.

As soon as the dark hedge enfolded her, she paused to catch her breath, but she didn't stay there. She waited until Nat joined her. Then she tunneled her way back to the sidewalk and set of at a brisk gallop down the street.

Nat ran to keep up with her. "Willow, wait."

She didn't even turn around. "We don't have time. We have to get back to the station and find Carl and Naya. I believe Jason is going to try something next, and we have to alert them."

"But Jason didn't kill Roy," Nat pointed out. "You just heard Annika admit to putting the fuel cartridge in the bakery. Annika, Josephine and Marlena all planned to kill Roy together."

Willow shook her head, but her thoughts were never more crystal clear. "Annika planted the fuel cartridge in the bakery, but she didn't start the fire."

"What makes you say that?" Nat asked.

"Don't you remember what Chester said?" Willow asked. "He said a regular flame wouldn't cause that cartridge to explode and set the bakery on fire. Whoever set that fire used military grade blasting caps to ignite the fuel."

"But we still don't know who that was," Nat pointed out. "Any one of those three women could have a military background."

Willow stopped and faced Nat. "Don't tell me the world-famous police cat didn't notice what was right there in front of his eyes in that house. Don't tell me little old Willow the house cat noticed something you didn't."

Nat frowned. "What are you talking about?"

"Didn't you bother to look around the house?"

Willow asked. "Didn't you look to see what sort of people lived there?"

Nat's whiskers twitched. "I don't know what you're talking about."

Willow started walking again. She answered Nat over her shoulder. "I was right about this neighborhood being familiar. I've been here before. In fact, I used to live here. Annika Neilsson was my old owner."

Nat stopped in his tracks. "What?"

Willow nodded, but she didn't stop walking. Every minute before they found Carl and Naya was a minute wasted. "I lived in that house. I know more about Jason Dempsey than anybody except maybe Annika herself. He was in the Marine Corps before he moved here. He was honorably discharged after serving five tours in Iraq, and he earned a whole pile of medals. He had them mounted in frames in the hall of that house, right in front of you, Nat."

Nat looked away. "That's impossible."

"It's the facts, Willow exclaimed. This was one big plot to kill Roy for his money and distribute it between the four of them. They were all in it together."

CHAPTER 11

Nat surveyed the surroundings. "How are we going to break the news to Carl and Naya?"

Willow surveyed the neighborhood from the movie theater roof. "I don't know, but we have to find a way to lead them in the right direction. How we will accomplish that, I have no clue."

"We've been standing here for fifteen minutes with no ideas," Nat pointed out. "Let's go back to the station. Something might turn up."

Willow sighed and started to turn away. All of a sudden, she stopped. "Nat, look."

In the distance, an unmarked cruiser turned into the street and stopped in front of the Nickel Alley Cafe. "They're here."

Nat looked around. "They must be coming to check on Jason's alibi. If Chester and Bella saw Josephine and Jason in the alley, maybe someone else did, too."

Willow sucked in her breath. When she spoke, she barely made any sound. "Nat."

He followed her gaze. "Well, what do you know about that?"

"What's he doing here?" Willow tiptoed to the roof edge and peered down at Jason from above.

He parked his car across the street and sat in the driver's seat for a moment. He scanned the alley, but he didn't see anything but a couple of cats hanging around the dumpster. He got out, looked both ways, and strode across the street.

"Let's get down there," Nat suggested. "Something tells me this is our chance."

They trotted down the stairs and paused at the top of the alley. Chester stuck his head out from under a pile of oily newspaper when Jason approached. Bella yowled and jumped up onto the window ledge. She perched between two clay flower pots and just managed to avoid knocking them off.

"Quick, Nat!" Willow whispered. "Run around to the cafe and find a way to bring Carl and Naya out here."

"How am I going to do that?" he asked.

"I have no idea," she replied. "I'm sure you'll

think of something."

Nat ran back the other way and disappeared. Willow ventured into the alley. Chester threw off his paper covering, and Bella smiled down at her. Jason paid the cats no attention. He hurried down the alley to another window near the ground level of a nearby building and started digging through the dirt. He brushed the soil off a stainless steel cylinder and shoved it into his pocket.

"Can I do anything for you, my dear?" Chester asked.

Willow kept her eyes on Jason. "I need your help, Chester. Carl and Naya are inside the cafe right now. We have to find a way to tip them off that Jason is right outside."

"How do you plan to do that?" Chester asked.

Willow hesitated just long enough to take her eyes off Jason. "I don't know. I was hoping you and Bella could help us."

"I'm not a police cat," Chester growled.

"What can we do to help?" Bella asked.

At that moment, a shout went up inside the cafe. The back door flew open, and voices echoed down the alley. "Get that cat out of here!"

Chester and Willow turned around to see Nat streaking through the cafe. He dodged between customers' legs and toppled chairs in his wake. Women screamed and startled patrons dropped their coffee cups. Broken crockery and steaming coffee covered the floor.

Carl and Naya looked up from their conversation with the clerk at the cash register. Carl stared at the unfolding pandemonium, but Naya gasped out loud. "That's Nat! What's he doing here?"

Nat never stopped running. Willow's heart soared at the sight of him. She would have called out encouragement to him, but she didn't want to distract him. He raced through the cafe with employees and the manager in hot pursuit.

Nat made a bee line for the back door and doubled his speed. He put the puddles of coffee and whipped cream behind him and dashed headlong through the door. The manager waved his arms one last time and shouted after him. The next minute, the door slammed shut and Nat vanished into thin air.

Carl bent over his wallet, but Naya stared at the closed door with a curious look on her face. Carl paid the tab, but when he looked up, he found Naya moving toward the back door in a stupefied trance.

"What are you doing?" Carl asked.

Naya didn't turn around. "That was Nat."

"So what?" Carl asked. "He probably gets up to all kinds of mischief when he leaves the station. He'll find his way back later."

Naya didn't turn around. The manager gave her a strange look of his own, but he wasn't going to stand in the way of a police investigation.

Naya pushed the door open, and her eyes popped. "Oh, hello, Jason. What are you doing here?"

Jason glanced around and attempted a feeble smile. "Hello, Detective. I dropped my keys here yesterday when I was here with Josephine. I came back to find them."

Carl stuck his head through the door. "What's going on?"

Willow watched the unfolding scene. Nat did his job to bring Carl and Naya out into the alley. Now she had to find a way to show them the cylinder in Jason's pocket.

Willow glanced up at Bella. She didn't have a moment to lose. She coiled every fiber in her body and launched herself up toward the ledge where the tiny cat sat. Time stood still, and no one on the ground even saw her jump.

She left the ground and sailed through the air in one perfect arc. She never understood before or since how she did it, but she touched down on the ledge next to Bella. She didn't bother to stay away from the flower pots, and there wasn't enough room on the ledge for her.

She found her footing on the window ledge and slithered behind the flower pots. She pushed them off the ledge, and they crashed to the ground in a spray of clay and dirt. Carl and Naya drew back to escape the rain of debris, but Jason saw his chance to make a clean get-away. He whirled away and set off for a run for his car.

He had a bad habit, though, of not noticing alley cats in inconvenient places. Chester only had to take one step to position his body in Jason's way, and the young man tripped over him and fell flat on his face at Carl and Naya's feet.

The detectives stared down at him. "Where are you going, Jason?" Naya asked.

Jason groaned and rolled over onto his back. Chester made a pretense of running away in fright.

Naya's eyes widened. "What's that in your pocket, Jason?"

He didn't answer, and he didn't bother to try to get away. He closed his eyes while Naya pulled the cylinder out of his pocket. She dumped the contents into her palm.

"Blasting caps," Carl exclaimed. "What's he doing with those?"

"Don't you remember?" Naya asked. "The crime lab turned up traces of these next to the fuel that started the fire. He must have used them to bypass the fuel cartridge safety device. It was in the lab report."

Carl pulled his head down between his shoulders. "Oh yeah. I remember."

In the next few moments, the detectives

listened as Jason confessed to the killing of Roy with the help of Annika, Marlena and Josephine. He told them how the four of them had conspired to kill Roy and split his estate. Naya and Carl took out their hand cuffs and placed them around Jason's wrists. They immediately contacted police headquarters to have the other three conspirators arrested.

Willow watched Carl shove Jason into the back of a squad car. Then she looked around the alley and found Nat sticking his nose out from behind the dumpster. "It's safe to come out now."

Nat sighed and stepped out into the alley. "Thank goodness that's over. I don't want to do that again in a hurry."

Willow laughed. "You sure got their attention. I've never seen a cat run so fast." She laughed at the memory of his wild race through the cafe."

He sat down and licked his shoulder. "You're the one who did all the hard work. You put all of the pieces of the puzzle together and sensed were Jason would be next. You made him trip over Chester so Naya would see the cylinder in his pocket. The other three women will serve their time as well. None of that would have happened if it wasn't for you. How does it feel to solve your first case?"

Willow swelled with pride. "It feels pretty good. So does this make me an official police cat?"

Nat fell in at her side on the way back to the station. "It's official. Now all you need is a badge."

THE END.

Thank you for purchasing, downloading and reading my book. I strive to create stories that my readers will love. If you enjoyed this book I would be very grateful if you posted a short review on Amazon.

Thank you for purchasing this book and thank you for your support.

For other books by Nancy C. Davis Visit:

Catcozymysteries.com

Nancy C. Davis

Your Free Gifts

Visit the Following link to Receive 3 Free Mini Cozy Mysteries

http://catcozymysteries.com/masp

Made in the USA
Columbia, SC
28 January 2019